The Hungry Princess & The One Legged Frog

A.M Dean

Illustrated by Cain Wheale

There once lived a hungry princess who was very lonely.
She loved to eat!
She had no one to play with or even to eat with.

Each day she grew sadder and sadder.
The sadder she felt the more she would eat

SHE ATE EVERYTHING! She ate every hour. She ate every minute.

On Monday she ate 5 pizzas.

On Tuesday she ate 6 cheeseburgers.

On Wednesday she ate 7 birthday cakes. It wasn't even her birthday!

On Thursday, she ate 8 sausages and eggs.

On Friday, she ate 9 strawberry tarts.

On Saturday, she ate 10 ice creams.

And on Sunday, she had a giant bowl of spaghetti!

That Sunday, the princess went out to play with her red ball. As she was playing, she heard a voice calling, "help me, help me!" The voice was coming from a well. "Hello?" called the princess.

She looked inside the well and saw a frog.
"Hello?" the princess called again.
"Hello, could you help me out, please?" asked the frog.

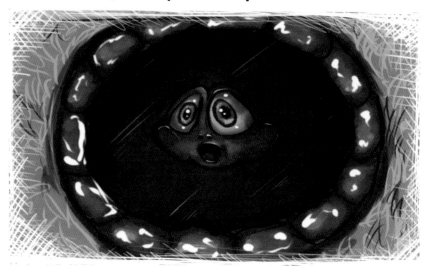

The princess helped the frog out of the well.
The frog was happy to get out of the well.

"Thank you!" said the frog,"I have been in that well
for a very long time!"
The princess was happy to help the frog.

Suddenly, the princess grabbed the frog and gave him a big kiss.
The frog was surprised and asked, "why are you kissing me?"

"Oh!" cried the princess, "I am a princess, and I thought you would turn into a prince! I have heard that frogs turn into handsome princes if kissed by a princess!"
"I am not a prince," said the frog.

The princess felt sad. She had hoped that he would turn into a prince. It is not every day you find a frog in a well!
The frog saw how sad the princess looked, and said,"Don't worry, we can be friends if you would like?"

The princess cheered up. "I would like to be your friend," she said.
They both played with the princess's favourite red ball.
They played and played until they both grew tired and very hungry.

The frog's tummy growled.
The princess's tummy growled louder.
"I am hungry!" said the princess.

The frog was hungry too.
"Come to my palace for dinner," said the princess

At the palace, they ate and ate and ate.

After eating, the princess yawned.
The frog yawned.
"Would you like to take a nap?" asked the princess.

"Yes, please!" said the frog.
They both took a nap in the princess' great big bed.

It was dark when the princess woke up. Her tummy started to growl.
The frog was still asleep. Her tummy growled louder.

There was no more food left in the kitchen. They had eaten it all!
Her tummy growled and growled, louder and louder!

The princess had a thought. She had heard that frogs taste quite delicious!
She looked at the frog.

Her tummy let off an even louder growl and then a deep rumble.
"Grrrrrrrrrrowl!" "Rrrrrrrrr!"

CRUNCH!

CRUNCH!

CRUNCH!

The next morning...there was a horrendous scream!

The frog cried out, "where is my leg?"
The princess woke up looking very guilty.

The princess had eaten the frog's leg!

"I am very sorry," sobbed the princess, "I was hungry, and my tummy wouldn't stop rumbling!" she sobbed even harder. She cried and cried.

The frog was very angry. The princess had eaten his leg!

The frog hopped on his one leg to escape. He hopped and hopped until he could hop no more. He came to a stream and sat down, very unhappy and very angry.

The princess called on everyone in the kingdom to help find the frog. But no one could find him.

The Princess went to find the frog all by herself. She did not find him. She came across a stream and sat down.

She had lost a good friend because of her greedy tummy.

She started to cry and called out loudly, "I am so sorry!"

The princess didn't see that the frog was watching from behind some bushes.

The frog saw how terribly sorry the princess looked. He remembered how the princess had helped him.

He felt sorry for the princess "don't worry!" said the frog, "I will forgive you if you promise never to eat me again."

The princess was so happy to see the frog and gave him a huge hug. "I won't eat you; I promise!" she sobbed.

The princess ordered her best carpenter to make the frog a wooden leg. It had the shiniest golden wheels!

From that day on, the princess never ate any more frogs. She ate less and less and was always careful about what she ate.

Every day, the princess and the frog played and played. They went on adventures, played with her red ball, and splashed in the pond.

They were happy, and everyone loved the frog's new leg.

The End.

Printed in Great Britain
by Amazon